DOOZERS

Stick
with It

™

adapted by Natalie Shaw
based on the screenplay written by Craig Martin

Ready-to-Read

Simon Spotlight
New York London Toronto Sydney New Delhi

SIMON SPOTLIGHT

An imprint of Simon & Schuster Children's Publishing Division

1230 Avenue of the Americas, New York, New York 10020

This Simon Spotlight edition August 2015

© 2015 The Jim Henson Company. JIM HENSON'S mark & logo, DOOZERS mark & logo, characters and elements are trademarks of The Jim Henson Company. All Rights Reserved.

All rights reserved, including the right of reproduction in whole or in part in any form.

SIMON SPOTLIGHT, READY-TO-READ, and colophon are registered trademarks of Simon & Schuster, Inc.

For information about special discounts for bulk purchases, please contact Simon & Schuster Special Sales at 1-866-506-1949 or business@simonandschuster.com.

Manufactured in the United States of America 0715 LAK

10 9 8 7 6 5 4 3 2 1

ISBN 978-1-4814-3218-4 (hc)

ISBN 978-1-4814-3217-7 (pbk)

ISBN 978-1-4814-3219-1 (eBook)

The Pod Squad is going

to the new Doozer Creek

playground.

"It looks awesome!"

Spike says.

But it is not finished.

They are here to help!

"Thanks, Pod Squad!"

says Professor Gimbal.

"First we can test

the rides!"

Molly Bolt and Flex

try the seesaw.

Daisy Wheel goes down

the slide.

Flex climbs the climbing wall.

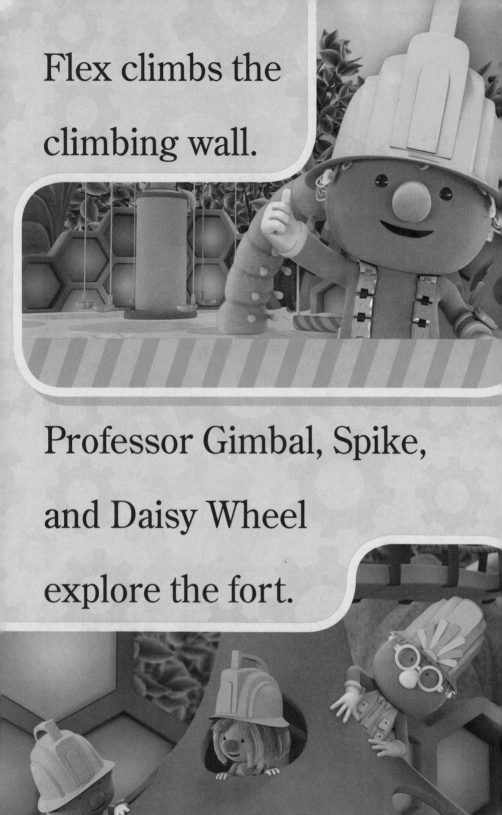

Professor Gimbal, Spike, and Daisy Wheel explore the fort.

"They all work great,"

Molly Bolt says.

"Now we need to finish

the bridge."

They work on the bridge.

Then they test it!

Daisy Wheel runs across

"The bridge might get

slippery in the rain,"

Spike says.

He wants to try his

new invention,

Super Sticking Spray!

He sprays the bridge.

"Perfect!" he says.

"What next?"

"The beetle blower!"
Professor Gimbal says.
"We have to attach the
beetle part to the tube.
Then we will be done!"

"Allow me," says Spike.

He uses his spray

to attach the part.

Then Spike tests it.

He jumps on the beetle,

sending air into the tube.

"This is fun!" he says.

"It may be fun,

but the part fell off!"

cries Molly Bolt.

Spike adds more spray.

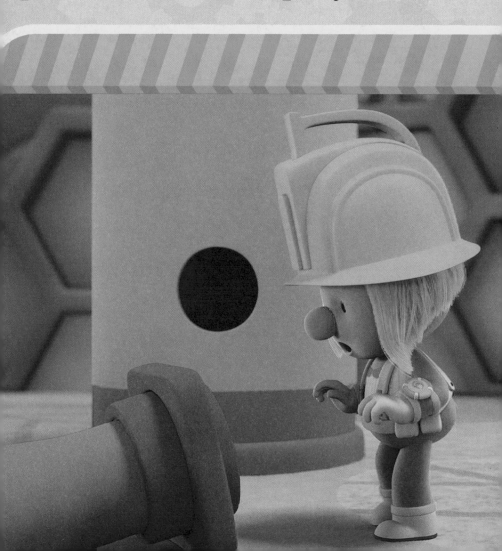

The part falls off again!

The spray starts off sticky,

but then it is slippery!

"This is why we test things,"

Professor Gimbal says.

Molly Bolt asks Spike,

"What else did you spray?"

Spike gasps. "The bridge!"

Professor Gimbal is

on the bridge!

"Careful!" they yell.

"It is slippery!"

Professor Gimbal slips
and lands in the fort.
"I am okay," he says,
"but I am stuck!"

The Pod Squad will help!

Spike tries pulling with

his Grabbers.

They are too strong!

"That is tight!"

says Professor Gimbal.

Next they try the crane.

The crane does not work!
It pulls the whole fort
off the ground!

Next they try pushing.

Nothing happens.

They look around for

more ideas.

Spike sees the bridge
and remembers his
Super Sticking Spray.
"It goes from sticky
to slippery!" he says.

"Maybe it will make

him slippery!" Spike says.

Flex sprays

Professor Gimbal.

This time when they push,

he slides out!

"Yahoo!" he yells.

"Great work!"

Spike thinks his spray

needs a new name.

Super Slippery Spray!

"Yay, Pod Squad!"

The Pod Squad cheers.